Our Little
Frankish Cousins
of Long Ago

By Evaleen Stein

Our Little Frankish Cousins of Long Ago

Table of Contents

Preface

The Frankish ruler, Charlemagne, was one of the greatest monarchs that ever lived. Great not merely because he was a victorious warrior and the kingdom he ruled was enormous, but rather because living as he did in a time when many of his people were lawless and ignorant, he saw clearly the worth of law and wisdom. He did all in his power to govern justly and to teach his people in all that best knowledge without which no nation can become truly civilized.

The world has never forgotten his great deeds, and deep in its heart it still cherishes him as one of its most honored heroes.

Many are the songs and legends that cluster about his name, and someday I hope you will read these, for I am sure you will enjoy them. Meantime, perhaps you may be interested in learning something of the home life of this hero, so let me introduce Our Little Frankish Cousin of Long Ago, for he spent quite a while as page in the royal palace and so ought to be able to give you some idea of what folks did there. At least he can show you what Frankish boys did,—and, I do hope you will like him!

EVALEEN STEIN

CHAPTER I: Rainolf and the Palace Pages

ONE summer afternoon, ever and ever and ever so long ago, along a crooked street in the old town of Aachen a boy was walking slowly. He held in his hands a half unrolled scroll of parchment covered with queer squares and circles and quantities of stars, and at these he was peering with an intent curiosity. Indeed, he was so absorbed in trying to make out the figures on the parchment that he forgot to notice where he was going; and presently tripping over a large stone projecting from the narrow ill-paved street, down he tumbled, sprawling plump into the midst of a family of little pigs that had been following their mother just ahead of him.

Instantly there was a tremendous squealing as the frightened little beasts scurried off in all directions, and mingling with their squeals rose a chorus of merry shouts of laughter from a group of boys coming from the opposite direction.

"Ho! Ho! Rainolf!" they cried. "What were you trying to do? Catch a little pig for the palace cooks?"

Meantime Rainolf, having scrambled to his feet, began ruefully to brush the dust from his tunic of white linen and his legs wrapped in strips of the same material cross-gartered with knitted bands of blue wool. One of the boys good-naturedly picked up his round blue cap, while another handed him the roll of parchment which had been the cause of his trouble. As the boy caught a glimpse of the tracings on the scroll, "Rainolf," he said, "I'll wager you have been to see Master Leobard the astrologer!"

"Yes," replied Rainolf, "he was a friend of my father, and mother said for me to go to see him when I came to Aachen. I hunted him up to-day, and he was very kind and made my horoscope for a present."

Here the boys gathered around Rainolf again as he unrolled his parchment, and they all looked it over trying to puzzle out its meaning. Now, a horoscope was a chart showing the position of the stars in the sky at the hour of a baby's birth; and from these the astrologer who made it, and who was supposed to know much about the stars and a good deal of magic besides, declared he could foretell the child's future. People who could afford it in those days liked to have these horoscopes made for their children; but if one did not happen to have it done when a baby it answered just as well later on to furnish the astrologer with the right dates. This was the way Master Leobard had made the one for Rainolf, who had been born twelve years before, in a castle some distance from Aachen whither he had lately been sent by his widowed mother so that he might be educated in the court of the great King Charlemagne who ruled the land.

As now the boys looked at the parchment, "Well," said one of them, "it's no use for us to try to make it out. What did Master Leobard say? Is your fortune good?"

"Yes, Aymon," answered Rainolf, "I think it's fairly good,—though he did say I would get some hard knocks now and then."

"So," laughed one of the boys, "I suppose you tumbled down just now because your stars said you had to!"

Rainolf smiled as he added, "At any rate, if I do get some knocks, he said I would be a good fighter and always conquer my enemies." And he drew himself up proudly.

"You are a good fighter now," said Aymon, his close friend, as he looked admiringly at Rainolf's straight figure and fearless face with its blue eyes and frame of flaxen hair.

"But," went on Rainolf, "he said there was something else I would like much better than fighting and that I would make a success of it, and that I would see something of the world." Just here the horoscope was cut short, as "Look out!" cried one of the boys, and they all hastened to flatten themselves against the wall of an old brown house in front of which they happened to be standing. For a cart was coming down the street, which was so narrow that anybody walking there had to get out of the way or else squeeze up against some of the brown-beamed wooden houses or dark little shops on either side.

Meantime the cart came trundling by. It was heavy and rudely built, its two wheels made from solid blocks of wood which had been hewn with an ax till they were tolerably round. The cart was drawn by a big white ox wearing a clumsy wooden collar; and his patient eyes scarcely blinked nor did he turn his head as the heavy wheels bumped and creaked over the uneven stones of the street. Beside the cart walked a bare-headed peasant with red hair and beard and wearing a tunic of coarse gray homespun, his legs wrapped in bands of linen criss-crossed around them and on his feet shoes of heavy leather.

"Good-day," said Rainolf as the man passed. But the peasant only turned his head and stared.

"Where are you going?" pursued another boy undaunted by his silence.

At this, "To the King's palace," muttered the peasant as he prodded the ox with a long goad he held in his hand.

The ox started, the cart gave a jerk, and "Squawk! Squawk!" came from a couple of geese within as with feet tied together they helplessly flopped against some bags of meal piled in front of them.

"Oh," said Aymon, standing on tiptoe trying to look into the cart, "never mind, Rainolf, that you didn't catch those little pigs! All these things are going to the palace kitchen!"

"Yes," put in another boy, pointing down the crooked street, "and there come a lot more!"

Sure enough, there were more ox-carts, and in between them even some flocks of sheep and a number of cattle. All these provisions the peasant folk had raised on the lands of the King near Aachen, and they were bringing them in, as they did once in so often, for the use of the large household at the palace. By and by, when these supplies were all eaten, the King and all the palace people would probably move off for a while to some other part of the kingdom where he had more farms to fill the royal larder.

As now the last cart went creaking along the street, "Where are you boys going?" asked Rainolf of the others, who, like himself, were all pages from the palace.

"Oh," said Aymon, "nowhere in particular. The King's chamberlain sent us to old Grimwald, the armorer, to see if he had finished some new boar-spears for the big hunt next week. The palace armorer has more than he can do, so Grimwald is helping him. But the spears were not done."

Meantime they all loitered along the street, now and then looking in the shops on either side. These were small and dark, more like little cubby holes than our idea of shops. There was no glass in their narrow windows, only heavy wooden shutters to be closed and barred at night. The shop-keepers sat on benches inside, most of them hard at work making their wares. There was the shoe-dealer sewing up shoes of thick leather cut in one piece soles and all, or, if one preferred, he had sandals of rawhide with leather thongs to tie them on. There was the cloth-seller, whose wife had spun and woven the woollen stuffs and the rolls of linen and narrow colored bands in which the Frankish men wrapped and cross-gartered their legs; for no one had thought of trousers or stockings. Then there was the silk-dealer, whose wares had come from the town of Lyons, and goldsmiths beating out trinkets of gold and silver for the noble ladies.

Past these was a many-gabled inn; for as Aachen was the King's capital, numbers of people came there on different errands. Across from the inn was a grassy square and a low brown house where on market days one might buy cheeses and chunks of meat and coarsely ground meal and a few kinds of vegetables and for sweetmeats cakes made of meal and honey, for nobody had heard of sugar.

Near the market-house a juggler was standing on his head, but only a few beggars and children were watching him; and as the boys went along they merely glanced at him with a scornful "Pooh! Does he suppose we can't stand on our heads, too?" For jugglers were plenty and this one not so clever as most.

Beyond the square was the shop of Grimwald, the armorer, whose swords and helmets and spears were the best in Aachen. Grimwald was busy making a suit of armor by sewing hundreds of small iron rings on a tunic of leather, and beside him an apprentice was sharpening the boar-spears as he turned a great grindstone. Standing close to this was an elfish figure in a bright yellow tunic, a little man, not more than four feet high, with a peaked face and strange deep eyes, now shrewd and keen, now twinkling and kindly.

"Ho!" cried one of the boys, looking into the shop, "there is the King's jester!" "Malagis," he called to the dwarf, "what are you doing in there?"

At this Malagis came out, limping a little because of one crooked foot; though it was astonishing how he could caper when he wanted to. "Oh," he said, "I was just standing by the grindstone a minute getting my wits sharpened. It would be good for all of you, too," he added, sweeping the group with a carved ivory staff he held, "only it would take so frightfully long!"

"One thing," said Aymon laughing, "you don't need to sharpen your tongue, Malagis!"

8

Here the dwarf prodded him with his staff, just as the peasants prodded their oxen, and began capering along beside the boys.

Soon they passed the row of shops and came to dwelling houses, some with upper stories and peaked roofs, some low and rambling. On nearly all heavy shutters stood open showing within sometimes richly dressed ladies and their maids spinning and weaving or embroidering, and sometimes women in homespun bending over pots and pans in which things were cooking at big fireplaces while puffs of smoke curled out through the windows till you would have been quite sure all those houses were afire! But the boys knew better and paid no attention, for nobody had chimneys, and smoke was expected to get out as best it could.

Presently, "I'll tell you what let's do!" cried Rainolf. "Let's go back to the palace swimming-pool and see if there is a chance for a swim!"

"All right!" echoed the rest, and off they scampered past the last straggling houses till they came to the edge of Aachen, and looming ahead rose the great palace of the mighty King Charlemagne. After the plain wooden houses of the old town, it would have made you blink to see how very large and fine was this palace with its stone walls and tall towers and its many porticoes and doorways and cornices all of beautifully carved marble. In the midst of it was a wide courtyard with grass and flowers and numbers of marble statues.

Not far from the palace, in a pleasant meadow-land, was a large pool lined with blocks of stone and divided into two parts, in one of which was warm and in the other cold water; for it was fed from springs nearby, and some of these always ran warm. Indeed, the chief reason why King Charlemagne had built one of his finest palaces here was that he might bathe often in these warm medicinal springs. He had had the swimming-pool made large enough, however, for others of his household to enjoy it as well; though the boys would not have presumed to go in if the King himself were there. But when they came up only a few soldiers and other humbler folk were swimming about, so all they had to do was throw off their tunics and jump in, and soon they were splashing around like a school of porpoises.

Presently Malagis, who had not hurried, came along by the pool and seeing Rainolf's parchment, which had fallen from his tunic and was about to tumble into the water, picked it up and placed a stone on it for safety, muttering as he did so, "There! One of those silly boys has been getting his horoscope! They're always in such a hurry to know their fortunes all at once,—as if they wouldn't find out soon enough anyhow! I could have told him myself, if I was a mind to, much better than old Master Leobard!" And Malagis poked the parchment contemptuously with his foot; for he was reputed something of a magician himself.

CHAPTER II: A Bit of History

NOW, while the boys are in swimming, suppose we stop a minute and answer a few questions. If you children would like to know when this story begins, you will have to subtract something over eleven hundred years from this year and that will leave you just three figures; which means that it was enormously long ago. For if you have subtracted right you will find that the story begins in the year 800. And if you want to know where the old town of Aachen was, you will have to turn in your geographies to the map of Europe and look in the western part of Prussia; and there you will find that Aachen, which is very near to France, has also a French name, Aix-la-Chapelle, which means Aachen of the chapel, or church, because of the wonderful one which King Charlemagne built there.

But if anybody had told Rainolf or Aymon or the rest of those boys in swimming that the town was ever called Aix-la-Chapelle and that it was in Prussia, they would have stared and laughed; for the simple reason that there wasn't any Prussia then. Neither was there any Germany or France as they are bounded in your maps, nor Belgium nor Holland.

"Dear me!" you say, "why what in the world *was* there?"

Well, there was just the same big country with its hills and valleys and mountains and rivers, only it wasn't all settled and divided up and named as it is now. It was all ruled by King Charlemagne, and, to be sure, some of it to the east of Aachen was vaguely called Germany, but nobody could have told exactly how far Germany went. While west and north and south of Aachen, where is now Belgium and Holland and France, was mostly called Gaul. In this great region many different kinds of people lived. Those in the southern part of Gaul were quite civilized, because once upon a time they had been conquered by the Romans who had taught them many things. Those up in the northern part of the kingdom were many of them still wild and savage; while those in the middle part were, as might have been expected betwixt and between; that is, civilized in many ways and in others very rude and ignorant.

A few hundred years before our story begins, when the whole country was peopled by wandering tribes generally fighting each other, one tribe, called the Franks, being stronger than the rest, managed to get possession of a large part of the land and a Frankish chief named Clovis became King. Clovis conquered many of the other tribes and added to his kingdom; and though he had been a heathen to start with, he ended by being baptized and becoming a Christian.

But Clovis seemed to be the only great chief of his family; for after he died his sons and grandsons and great- great- grandsons were all so stupid and good-for-nothing that the Frankish people did not know what to do with them. They did not like to take their crowns away from them, so they let them still be called Kings, but shut them up in their palaces or sometimes even carted them off to farmhouses in the country. And while each "Sluggard King," for so they were nick-named, thus dawdled away his life, the kingdom was really managed by a man called the Mayor of the Palace.

By and by there was a Mayor of the Palace named Pepin who was a very clever man and decided to make a change. He thought that as all the descendants of Clovis were too silly to rule and other people had to do all their work for them, it was high time to stop pretending they were Kings. By this time all the Frankish people had grown very tired of the foolish old royal family and quite agreed with Pepin. They said that as he had been such a good Mayor of the Palace he should be King instead of Childeric, who was the last of the family of Clovis and who was then shut up in a farmhouse where he did nothing but eat and drink and doze.

So the big Frankish warriors lifted Pepin up on their shields and showed him to everybody as their new King; and a very good one he made.

But it was Pepin's baby boy Charles who was destined to be the lasting glory of the Franks. When he grew up and inherited the kingdom, he soon earned the title of Charles the Great, or Charlemagne, which is the same thing. He extended his dominions till his kingdom spread over all that is now France and Germany and most of Italy and much more besides and was one of the largest in the world; and not only was he a great warrior, but he was one of the very greatest and wisest rulers the world has ever seen. Indeed, he was so remarkable and so powerful that it is no wonder that for hundreds of years after his time people declared that he was at least ten feet tall, that in battle he could hew down dozens of his enemies at a single stroke, and that he was so wise that he knew instantly everything that went on in the farthest parts of his kingdom.

Yes, about Charlemagne and the Twelve Paladins, who were his bravest warriors, more wonderful stories have been told and more beautiful songs sung than about any other King that ever lived, excepting only King Arthur of Britain and the Knights of the Round Table; and, of course, you have heard of them.

Now, Charlemagne was indeed very wise; and among other things he saw that the Franks had much to learn in many ways. And this brings us back to the King's palace; for he knew one thing particularly his people had to be taught, and that was how to build beautiful houses such as he had seen in his wars in Italy and other far countries. So when he wanted to build the palace at his favorite Aachen he brought home with him not only Italian workmen to teach the Franks, but also quantities of fine marble columns and handsome mosaics and beautiful carvings.

And that was why the great palace there was one of the finest of the many belonging to Charlemagne. And that was why, too, the big swimming-pool was so well made; for the King had seen baths like it at Rome.

But really it is time Rainolf and all those other boys came out of it, for they have been swimming all the while we have been talking about the Frankish people! And, besides, Charlemagne himself has not yet come into the story, and surely you must want to see what such a wonderful King is like.

So splash! out come the boys and run off to put on their clothes, and—if you look sharp—you will see the mighty Charlemagne come into the very next chapter; though he will come quietly and not as if he were entering a captured city. When he did that people used to be terribly frightened; for marching before him would be such multitudes of soldiers with iron spears and coats of iron mail and iron leggings, and so many bold knights on horseback, wearing iron armor and iron helmets and iron breastplates and iron gauntlets and carrying iron battle-axes, and then the mighty Charlemagne himself clad in iron from head to toe, riding an iron gray horse, holding in one hand an enormous iron lance, and looking so—but let us wait till he comes into the story.

13

CHAPTER III: The Palace School

THE next morning rather early, as usual, Rainolf and the other boys tumbled out of their beds in the wing of the palace where they slept, and as soon as they were dressed they ran out into the courtyard and began jumping over each other, for all the world like leap-frog! So that must have been it. By and by, "I'm hungry!" cried Aymon.

"So am I!" said Rainolf. "Let's find something to eat!"

And they all trooped off to the great palace kitchen where the cooks gave them some bread and cold meat and cheese, which they stood around and ate wherever they were not too much in the way. For breakfast was not made much of by anybody, nor set out except for the more important people of the palace. And it was never much like our breakfasts. There was always a great deal of meat for food, and for drink there was mead and wine. It had not occurred to people in those days that it might be agreeable to eat different kinds of things at different meals. And, besides, even if they had thought of it, they couldn't make their breakfasts very different from their dinners, because none of the Franks had ever heard of such things as rolled oats or puffed rice or coffee or griddle-cakes and maple syrup, poor things!

Nevertheless, when the boys had finished munching down their meat and bread they began, just as you do, to think about school.

"Rainolf!" said Aymon, "if you spell the rest of us down again to-day or get more good marks in grammar, I'll fight you!" But as he laughed good-naturedly as he made this threat, Rainolf laughed too. "Never mind," he answered, "maybe you won't have to! I think to-day's lesson will be a good deal harder than yesterday."

By this time they all decided that they had better be starting: so they made their way, not to the old town of Aachen, but across the courtyard to another part of the palace. Entering a handsome doorway and passing through a long corridor they came to a large room with a ceiling supported by many pillars and a floor of beautiful mosaics which the king had brought from Italy along with the rich tapestries which hung on the walls. At one side of the room was a raised platform, or dais, on which stood two throne-like chairs; while down the length of the floor below were a number of carved wooden benches.

When Rainolf and the rest of the pages entered they found a group of other boys and a few little girls already there. These were mostly children of the common soldiers and humbler folks about the palace. And, besides these, were quite a number of grown people, too, many of them noble ladies and gentlemen. The latter were dressed in linen tunics with sword-belts, and leg wrappings cross-gartered in bright colors, and all had long mustaches and shaven chins and hair nearly reaching their shoulders. The ladies wore silken tunics edged with embroidery, and trailing skirts, and on their heads embroidered scarfs arranged in folds covering their hair and with the long ends hanging down or else wrapped closely about their white throats.

Presently there was a hush, and everybody stood back and bowed very low as a group of people was seen coming toward the open door. Look sharp now, for here comes Charlemagne!

Rainolf fairly held his breath and stared with all his eyes as the stately figure drew near; for he had been in the palace only a short time and had seen but little of the King whose many affairs of state and various wars kept him often away from Aachen. Rainolf had heard so much of the great deeds of Charlemagne, how six Kings called themselves his vassals, and how his fame was known and talked of all the way from Bagdad to Britain, that to the boy he seemed quite like the hero of some wonder tale,—as indeed he was!

As now the great King entered the schoolroom he smiled pleasantly at the people there, and as he crossed over to take his place in one of the throne-like chairs on the dais, one might see that he was about fifty-five years old, and though not ten feet tall he was very near a good seven, and bore himself with royal dignity.

Circling his noble dome-like head was a gold and jeweled crown and beneath it hung rather long locks of iron gray hair, while over his breast flowed a long gray beard. His large blue eyes were bright and sparkling and his face wore a kindly but determined expression.

His dress was very simple; for the King loved the old Frankish costume of his people and only on very grand occasions would he consent to wear the splendid jeweled robes which belonged to his station. On this day he wore, as usual, a plain tunic of white linen with a silken hem of blue and girt with a sword-belt of interlaced gold and silver from which hung a sword with hilt and scabbard of the same precious metals. A square sea-blue mantle was fastened over one shoulder with a golden clasp and on his feet were leather shoes laced with gold cords over white leg-wrappings cross-gartered well above the knees with narrow bands of purple silk.

Beside Charlemagne, on the other tall chair, sat his Queen Luitgarde, while several of the princesses, his daughters, took their places near by; his sons would have been there, too, but they happened to be off fighting in a distant part of the kingdom. The noble ladies and gentlemen seated themselves on the benches nearest the dais, while Malagis perched on its edge looking very wise. Last of all, the palace pages and other children sat down on the farther benches.

Presently a young man entered, and, bowing before Charlemagne, laid on his knees a large parchment book.

"That's Master Einhard, the King's scribe. I guess you haven't seen him before; he's been sick since you came," whispered Aymon to Rainolf, as the young man seated himself on the edge of the dais near Malagis and took from the bosom of his tunic a tablet of parchment and a goose-quill pen ready to write down anything the King might wish.

"The King thinks a great deal of him," went on Aymon, "and he does of Master Alcuin, too. Look, there he comes now!"

Every one looked toward the tall man entering the room. He wore a monk's hood and robe, and in the cord that bound the latter at the waist were stuck some goose-quill pens and the hollow tip of a cow's horn filled with ink. This monk, who was the teacher, bowed respectfully to the King and Queen, took his place in the middle of the floor and school began.

Now if you think that the great Charlemagne and Queen Luitgarde and all the other ladies and gentlemen had come simply to visit this palace school, you are very much mistaken! No, indeed! They were all there to study just as hard as Rainolf and Aymon and all the other boys and girls.

For you must know that before the time of Charlemagne the Frankish people had no schools, and most of them knew just about as little of books and such things as reading, writing, and arithmetic and spelling and geography as they could possibly get along with; and that was very little indeed. But the wise King had done his best to change all this. All through the country there were many monasteries, and in these he had established schools so that the monks (who were about the only people then who could read or write) might teach the children of both rich and poor. And even in his own palace Charlemagne had for nearly twenty years kept up a school taught by the best scholars in the world, and in it he himself and the princes and princesses and many other grown folks of his household were not ashamed to sit with the children and study as hard as any of you boys and girls do now. But Sh! for, as I told you, the school had begun.

Everybody was still as a mouse; only Charlemagne spoke. "Master Alcuin," he said, "I would have you explain some points of grammar which I do not understand," and he looked with a perplexed air at the parchment book on his knees.

The monk stepped to the King's side and in a low tone cleared up the passage which puzzled him. Soon Charlemagne closed the book and said again, "Master Alcuin, pray tell us something of the courses of the stars at this season."

For Charlemagne was always deeply interested in the sky and used often to watch the stars for hours at night from the top of one of the highest palace towers.

Master Alcuin, as he was bidden, gave a little talk on astronomy; then going to an oaken table near by and taking a number of little books, almost like primers, written by hand on parchment, he gave them to the children to study.

"Aymon," whispered Rainolf softly to his friend who sat next to him, "did you say Master Alcuin made these books himself?"

"Yes," whispered Aymon, "he wrote them all out for us to use in the school."

The books were not so easy to learn from, either, even if they were primers; for all were in Latin. That was because the Frankish people had been fighting so long trying to make a nation of themselves that they had neither time nor learning to write books in their own language, which was still unfinished, and nobody was quite sure about its spelling or grammar. But the Greek and Latin people had been wise and civilized long before, while the Franks were still wild barbarians, and had written many wonderful books which had been carefully copied by monks and handed down in writing as there were no printing presses yet. It was from some of these that Master Alcuin had written the Latin books for the palace school.

17

As the children were puzzling over their lessons, presently he began asking them questions. And then Malagis, as he sometimes did when no one was looking, darted from his seat on the dais and hovered about slyly poking with his ivory wand any boy or girl who looked sleepy or wasn't paying attention; for a jester always did pretty much as he pleased and nobody dared complain.

I have no idea just what Master Alcuin's questions were about, but very likely it was grammar and spelling and arithmetic. At any rate, Rainolf was able to give more right answers than anybody else, and Aymon, sitting beside him, began to nudge him warningly. But Rainolf only nudged back and went on answering as many more as he could; for he had always been anxious to learn, and before coming to Aachen had studied hard at a little monastery school near his home castle.

While the boys and girls were having their lesson the grown folks were all busy with their own books. But soon the King, who was always interested in how things went on in his school, noticed Rainolf and quietly listened as the boy, with bright eyes and eager face, modestly answered Master Alcuin's questions. And after a while, when the school was dismissed for the day, before Charlemagne passed out he looked toward the boys' bench and beckoned to Rainolf.

Rainolf was so surprised and abashed that he blushed and stared and stood as if rooted to the spot.

"Go on, booby!" whispered Aymon anxiously, giving him a hurried push.

At this Rainolf suddenly plunged forward, and gathering his wits together managed to bow respectfully as he stood before the King, though he was trembling with excitement and his knees fairly knocked together.

"Lad," said the King, smiling at his embarrassment, "I liked the way you answered Master Alcuin's questions. I wish all my subjects would try as hard to learn something!" And the great King sighed; for above all things he longed to civilize his people and teach them the world's best knowledge. Then, suddenly extending his hand to the boy; "Child," he said, "you shall be one of my own pages. You remind me of Master Einhard when he was a boy in this same school. Where did you come from?"

YOU SHALL BE ONE OF MY PAGES.

"Sir," said Rainolf faintly, at last finding his tongue, "my home is Castle Aubri, on the Meuse river. My father was Count Gerard. He was killed in your last war with the Saxons. Mother sent me here a week ago so I might go to the palace school."

"That was right," said Charlemagne. "You have brave blood in your veins, boy. I remember your father well; he was a gallant soldier and a loyal subject. When we go to the banquet hall come up and stand near me. You shall be my cup-bearer instead of Charloun, who is a stupid lad." And the king left the room with Master Alcuin and the others.

CHAPTER IV: Dinner

WHEN the King passed on, Rainolf stood quite bewildered at his sudden advancement; though he could not help but wonder how it would suit Charloun, a fat dull-faced boy who had been made cup-bearer because his father was a powerful noble.

And he did not have to wait long to see. For Charloun had noticed the King talking to Rainolf and as now the latter was alone for a moment, he marched up to him demanding angrily "What did the King say to you?"

Rainolf drew himself up haughtily as he answered, "I don't know that it's any of your business, Charloun! Though," he added, "perhaps it is a little, seeing that he told me I am to be cup-bearer instead of you."

At this Charloun's dull face flushed with rage and he half doubled up his fist to strike Rainolf. But Rainolf, who was watching him, looked him straight in the eye, and "Be careful!" he warned. "This is no place to fight! But if you want to come out doors and do it, I am ready whenever you are."

Charloun, who was at heart a coward, dropped his fat fist and began to think he was not so anxious for a fight after all. And, the truth was, he was really relieved to be rid of the office of cup-bearer as several times Charlemagne had asked him questions about his lessons which he was quite unable to answer. So, muttering to himself, he stalked off; and Rainolf watching him smiled, for he knew Charloun was much more interested in the fact that it was nearly dinner-time than in his lost honors.

Meantime in the great banquet hall near the schoolroom long tables were set, the one for the royal family being placed on a dais at the upper end of the room. There were no cloths on these tables which were all made of polished boards laid over trestles, but on the royal one and those for the many noble ladies and gentlemen of the household were fine silver plates and gold and silver cups and flagons. There were neither forks nor spoons, however, only knives, which were needed to cut the meat of which there was always a great supply, and this and the other things people were expected to eat with their fingers. At the lower end of the hall were tables for the humbler palace folks, who had only wooden plates and great earthenware platters for their meat.

Rainolf had come into the hall while things were being made ready, and as he stood quietly watching them he thought how different was the great palace, with its handsome rooms and all the gold and silver dishes from his own home. His father's castle, like those of most of the Frankish nobles through the country, was just a big wooden house built around a square courtyard and protected outside by a palisade of roughly hewn logs and a moat beyond that. To be sure, there were many things going on within the wooden walls of the big rambling house. His father had had his own armorer; there was a stable for his war horses; there was a small mill where they ground the grain raised by the peasants on the castle lands; there were rooms where his mother and her maids spun and wove and embroidered;— though as Rainolf looked at the wonderful tapestries hanging on the palace walls he could not but admit they were more beautiful than those his mother had so carefully made for their home and which he had always before thought the finest in all the world. And then the dishes at home were just great wooden bowls with only a few silver and copper flagons,—but never mind, for dinner was ready and all the palace folks were taking their places.

Rainolf, as he had been bidden, came and stood near the chair of Charlemagne. Though it seemed strange to him to be so close to the great King, yet he was not so awkward in his new place as he had been used to waiting on his father in the same way.

Meantime, Aymon and the other pages busied themselves bringing in food for the royal table and those of the nobles. The boys only carried the dishes, for the carving and serving of them was an honor belonging to the high-born young men.

"Boy," whispered one of these, a tall handsome youth standing near Rainolf, "take that golden flagon and fill the King's cup with wine."

Rainolf hastened to do as he was told, and lifting in both hands the beautiful golden cup richly chased with figures of saints and circled with precious stones, he sank on one knee, as his father had taught him, and held it up to the King, who received it graciously, barely tasted it, and set it down by his plate. And Rainolf found that being cup-bearer for Charlemagne was not very hard work, as he took only three sips of wine all through the dinner. Wine was then the common drink, but the King despised drunkenness and always set the example of taking but little.

Neither was the dinner elaborate, for Charlemagne liked simple things, and, best of all, the roasted pheasants and hares which presently two hunters came bringing in piping hot and still on the long iron spits on which they had been cooked at the kitchen fireplace. These were carved and placed on the King's plate by the young Frankish noble who served also Queen Luitgarde and a tall man in rich priestly robes who sat at the King's left. This was the Archbishop of the Aachen cathedral, and near him was the teacher Master Alcuin; for Charlemagne always delighted to honor religion and learning.

At the royal table also sat young Master Einhard who smiled kindly at Rainolf, who colored and smiled back; for the two seemed drawn to one another, and, indeed, were to become close friends in spite of the difference in their ages. Next to Master Einhard the dwarf Malagis perched on his own special chair, and now and then catching Rainolf's eye he would give him so droll a wink that the boy could hardly keep his face straight; and he did not dare to laugh for all through dinner everybody kept very still because at one side of the hall a brown-robed monk was standing holding in his hands a parchment book from which he read aloud in Latin.

The book was a beautifully painted copy of "The City of God," written by the good Saint Augustine. Rainolf was not yet far enough along in his studies to understand it very well, and very likely most of the other people in the room were in the same case; but he noticed that Charlemagne listened attentively and seemed greatly to enjoy it, for he understood Latin and liked always to be read to while he ate.

Presently, however, the reading and dinner both came to an end; the latter finishing with large baskets of apples and cherries which were passed around to every one.

When the King left the hall it was to go, as usual, straight upstairs to his sleeping-room where he took off his clothes and went to bed for a couple of hours. Charlemagne counted much on this after-dinner nap, for his life was busy and full of care and he was but a poor sleeper at night. So hush, everybody!

CHAPTER V: Malagis and the Boys

"RAINOLF," said Aymon as the two boys went out into the courtyard after they had had their dinner, "while the King is sleeping, let's get the other boys and go over to the forest and see if there is anything in our rabbit snares."

"All right!" said Rainolf, and soon the group of pages left the palace and crossing a few open meadows came to the edge of the great wild forest that stretched on and on, nobody knew how far.

Here the boys scattered for awhile hunting the traps which several of them had placed there. But the little forest creatures had all been too wary for them and none had been caught. So by and by, answering Rainolf's halloo, they all came out and, as the air was heavy and warm under the dense boughs, were glad to throw themselves on the grass beneath a great oak tree which stood near a bubbling spring. This spring was thought to have miraculous power, but many people who visited it were afraid of witches and fairies whom they thought lived in the forest beyond; so as charms against these they often brought little silver trinkets, a number of which dangled from the boughs of the oak. The spot was a favorite lounging place for the boys, and this time they found some one ahead of them.

"Look!" said Aymon, "There's Malagis! I wonder if he thinks he can straighten his crooked foot by hanging it in the spring?"

"Tut! Tut!" said Malagis, who had heard them, "I'm not so silly! I'm just poking up these bubbles with my toes to see if there are really fairies playing ball with them as some people say."

"You had better be careful," said Aymon seriously, "They might not like your impudence."

"Pshaw!" retorted Malagis, taking care however to remove his foot, "I'm not afraid of fairies,—or witches either!" he added loftily. "I guess I know a few spells myself."

Here the boys looked at him respectfully and with some awe; for while he liked to chaff with them and allowed them to be very familiar with him, nevertheless everybody declared Malagis was a master of magic arts.

"Well," said one of the boys, after a pause, "maybe the King will let you work your spells, because you're his dwarf; but I heard one of the officers of the palace say the other day that Charlemagne had made a new law forbidding anybody to practice witchcraft."

At this Malagis looked very wise, but merely said, "That doesn't hurt me any. I'm not a witch! Though there are plenty of them in yonder forest!" and he nodded his head toward the dark trees behind them.

The boys shivered a little and drew closer together; for most people then believed in witches and fairies and dragons, too, for that matter. More than once it had been whispered that firebreathing dragons were to be found in some of the rocky caverns hidden among the trees.

"Malagis," said Rainolf, as he peered into its shadows, "how far does the forest reach?"

"Oh," answered the dwarf vaguely, "ever and ever and ever so far! Leagues and leagues and leagues; I dare say it's part of the big forest where Charlemagne overthrew the Irminsul."

"What was that?" asked one of the other boys.

"Why," said Malagis, "it was the special idol of the Saxon folks. You know they are the wild heathen tribes up north of here that tie their hair up in top-knots and carry great wooden clubs, and that Charlemagne has been fighting for years and years trying to conquer and make Christians of."

"Well, the thing they called the Irminsul was a big wooden pillar set up in a certain place in the forest and on top of it was an image of a man wearing a helmet and carrying a shield with a bear and lion carved on it. There were great treasures of gold and jewels at the foot of the pillar, offerings from the Saxons; for the Irminsul was their most sacred idol."

"And did you say Charlemagne threw it over?" put in Aymon.

"Indeed he did!" answered Malagis. "He marched up there with his army and hunted through the forest till he found where it was. Of course the Saxons rushed out all ready to fight, but then they felt sure the idol would do something terrible to the King and save them the trouble. So they stood around waiting for it to happen."

"But that didn't bother Charlemagne a bit. He defied them. And then instead of the Irminsul doing anything, he simply walked up to it and knocked it over and smash! down it tumbled and broke all to pieces! After that he burned up the wooden pillar and took the treasures and divided them among his bravest captains."

"What did the Saxons say to that?" asked Rainolf.

"Well," said Malagis, "at first they were stunned; but they still had hopes of revenge. For it seems the King's army had had to march a long way without any water, and the Saxons saw the Franks were half dead from thirst and thought they would all die entirely in a few minutes and that that was the way the Irminsul meant to punish them."

"But, bless your heart," went on Malagis chuckling, "just then along came a big black cloud and when it got right over Charlemagne's army what did it do but burst and pour down buckets and buckets-full of water, so they had all they could drink and more, too! When the Saxons saw that, they were as meek as could be and all said they would submit to the King and be Christians. And there were so many that it kept Archbishop Turpin and all the priests who were along with Charlemagne busy for three days baptizing them. Of course more of the heathen ones keep cropping up now and then for the King to fight, but he has them very well under control now."

"The King is surely a great warrior!" said Rainolf.

"Yes," said Malagis, "but he's greater still at making good laws and seeing that people mind them. He's great on learning, too. That's why, years ago, he sent all the way to Britain for Master Alcuin to come over and start the palace school; he wanted his children and everybody's children to learn something. You boys are lucky to have Master Alcuin teach you awhile, for he is a famous scholar."

"Why, won't he teach us all the time?" asked Rainolf.

"No," said Aymon, "didn't I tell you that three years ago the King gave him the Abbey at Tours and he has started another big school there?"

"Yes," said Malagis, "he is just here now because the King wanted to consult him about something."

"Who will teach us when he goes back?" again asked Rainolf.

"Probably that big sandy-haired monk who sat to-day near Master Einhard," said Malagis, "Did you notice him?"

"No," said Rainolf, who had been rather bewildered by the number of grown people in the school.

"Well," said Malagis, who was in a talkative mood, "it's funny how he got here. One day, about two years ago, I was going along the street in Aachen, and when I came to the marketplace there on a bench stood that monk and another one like him, both Scotch though they had come here from Ireland. They were both crying out at the top of their lungs, 'Knowledge to sell! Knowledge to sell! Who'll buy?' for all the world like a couple of fish-mongers."

"I thought it so odd, that when I got back to the palace I told Charlemagne and he sent for them to come to him. He asked them if it was true they were trying to hawk knowledge as if it were a brace of pigeons, and they said yes, it was; that they had first-rate knowledge to sell to the highest bidder. The King was pleased with them, and amused, too, I think. Anyway, he engaged them for teachers, and they proved to be fine. One of them is off now starting more schools."

"Does Master Einhard teach?" asked Rainolf, who wanted to know who everybody was.

"No," said Malagis, "he has about all he can do as the King's scribe; though he is a mighty good minnesinger besides and often sings in the evenings. He was taught in the palace school with the King's children and always stood so high in his studies that Charlemagne noticed him and has shown him great favor."

"You were lucky, boy," continued the dwarf, eying Rainolf shrewdly, "to attract the King's attention to-day. It's the good scholars that always get his help. Do you know what he did not long ago?"

"No," said Rainolf wonderingly.

"I will tell you," said Malagis, clasping his hands around his knees on which he rested his peaked chin. "He was on his way home from the town of Paderborn and stopped for dinner at the monastery of Saint Martin, and after dinner went in to look at the monastery school. About half the children there came from noble families and lived in castles, and the rest were just poor children from the village of Saint Martin. The King began asking questions, and it seems all the noble children had been spending their time playing and paying no attention to the monks; so just about all the answers he got came from the poor children who were used to minding and did what they were told and studied their books.

"Charlemagne was very angry. He quickly sorted out all the poor children and put them at his right hand and praised them and spoke kindly to them. And then he turned around and if he didn't give those noble children the worst lecture they ever got!"

Here Malagis pursed up his lips and smiled as he went on, "He told them they would be terribly fooled if they thought because their fathers were noblemen they could have honors whether they knew anything or not. He said he would show his favor to the people who were learning things, no matter how poor they were, and if those noble children expected to get anything from him they would have to start in and do some studying."

Here some of the boys who had not been getting on much at the palace school, began to look very uncomfortable, and one of them hastened to change the subject. "Malagis," he said, pointing to one of the high towers of the palace not far away, "is that really a brazen eagle there on top of the tower? It is so high up I can't see it very well."

"And," said another boy, "is it true that sometimes it turns by magic, and that then the King knows that he is needed in whatever part of kingdom the eagle seems to look toward?"

"Yes," answered Malagis gravely, "it is quite true. I helped to place that eagle myself!" and he wagged his head proudly. "You just keep watch of it,"—here Malagis crumpled his claw-like hands into a sort of funnel through which his keen eyes peered at the eagle as he went on slowly,— "it's beginning now to turn—just the least—little tiny bit— to the south!"

"What does that mean?" asked the boys eagerly. "What is south of here?" For none of them knew much geography; nor did anybody else, for that matter. You would have laughed to see their maps and wondered how anyone found his way about at all.

"Hm," said Malagis sagely, "there is a great deal south of us. There is Burgundy and Africa and Spain and a great deal of Asia and the kingdom of Prester John,"—which most people thought was a wonderful place, somewhere to the southeast, where there were red and blue lions and many marvelous things. So Malagis supposed he was telling the truth, as also about Asia; but then he came back to facts when he added, "Yes, and there's

Italy and Rome where the Pope lives. I wouldn't wonder if the eagle is going to mean Italy."

Here a little group of Aachen folk came bringing a blind man to the spring so that he might bathe his eyes in its miraculous waters. And the boys and Malagis slowly strolled off toward the palace.

CHAPTER VI: A Boar Hunt and a Music Lesson

IT was the day of the great boar hunt for which spears and knives had been sharpening for at least a week. Everybody had been up since dawn and the palace courtyard rang with the neighing of horses and the baying of hounds. Presently the king appeared, his blue eyes sparkling and eager; for hunting was his favorite sport. Indeed, the great wild forest full of wild beasts to be chased was, next to the warm springs, the chief reason why he had built his finest palace at the edge of Aachen.

Soon Charlemagne had mounted a splendid black horse which had been pawing the ground impatiently as a young Frankish noble clung to the bronze chains which served for bridle and which he now handed over to the King as the latter arranged himself on the handsomely carved leather saddle. He was dressed as usual, save that stuck through his sword-belt shone a long knife with a jeweled handle, while slung over one shoulder was a silver chain from which hung his hunting horn. It was made from the horn of an ox, the broad end being finished with a band of silver on which were chased hounds running at full speed.

The young Frank next handed the King a long, polished boar-spear, and at this signal all the other huntsmen sprang to their saddles, seized their spears from the attendants, the packs of hounds were turned loose, and Clatter! Clatter! Clatter! Thud! Thud! Thud! Bow-wow! Wow-wow-wow! Brrh-rrh! off they rushed toward the great forest.

On, on they pelted, across the meadows, toward the tall trees; and once within their shadows little they cared whether witch or fairy crossed their path. For the one thought of all those headlong huntsmen was for their bellowing hounds to start up some one of the fierce wild boars from his forest lair, so that they might chase him as with quivering bristles and red burning eyes he flew before them.

As Rainolf and the other boys, who had been in the courtyard watching the hunt start, heard the last echoes die away in the forest they all sighed enviously, and "Oh," said Rainolf, "don't I wish they'd have let us go along!"

IT WAS THE DAY OF THE GREAT BOAR HUNT.

All the rest felt quite the same way about it; for they had been taught to ride and could shoot very well with their bows and arrows, though, of course, they could not handle spears as yet. As they turned around with long faces, they were only half consoled when Aymon said, "Well, one comfort, Master Alcuin says we are to have a half holiday and need only take our singing lesson over in the cathedral."

So in a little while they all went over to the great cathedral which the King had caused to be built near the palace. It was very beautiful, being patterned after one Charlemagne had seen in Italy; and, as for the palace, he had brought wonderful Italian marbles and mosaics for it. Inside, in the place for the choir, was a carved wooden rack which held a very large parchment book. Its open pages were covered with bars of music made big enough so a number of singers could stand in front of it and yet be able to see the notes; for books were too scarce for everybody to have one.

When the boys entered the cathedral a row of men were already ranged in front of the choir book, among them Master Einhard, who smiled at Rainolf and made room for him beside himself as the other boys took their places behind, peering at the book as best they could. Facing them all stood the black-eyed teacher whom Charlemagne had brought from Italy to show the Frankish singers how properly to chant the church service and also to instruct the children in music.

As now the Italian beat time with one hand and sang "do-re-mi-fa," he frowned at the untrained voices of the Franks; that is, all but Master Einhard and Rainolf. These two had very sweet voices which blended well together; and as Rainolf stood beside Master Einhard he felt that he would rather sing beautifully than to do almost anything else, and he wondered if this was what Master Leobard meant when he said there would be something he would care more for than being a warrior. "Yes," he said to himself, "if I could only sing and make up songs of my own like Master Einhard does! And I will some day!" For, as Rainolf sang, a power began to waken within him.

Meantime, the Italian teacher fairly wrung his hands as the other singers went on do-re-mi-fa-ing without the least idea how badly they were doing it. And soon another sound arose which was almost as bad as their singing. It was the cathedral organ, which a young Frank was playing while another strapping youth puffed and panted as he worked a large bellows by which he forced the air into its few brass pipes. The keys were wide and heavy, and the young Frank in front of them struck each one a resounding blow with his fist, as that was the only way anybody could play on them.

Nevertheless, this organ which was the first any of the Frankish people had seen, was considered very wonderful indeed, and had been sent all the way from Constantinople as a present from the Greek emperor. And only the Sunday before, a noble Frankish lady had actually fainted from sheer joy at hearing so marvelous a musical instrument! So, you see, you really had better not laugh at it nor at the young Frank cheerfully pounding away with both fists.

The choir singers and the boys listened to the organ with great respect, as they had been taught, and supposed of course it must be very grand. Still, most of them felt relieved when the music lesson was over and they went out into the quiet morning air.

In the cathedral porch was a stone seat; and here as the boys passed along they saw Malagis curled up beside an old man wrapped in a long mantle and holding on his knees a musical instrument which looked something like a fiddle.

"I wonder where Malagis picked up that minnesinger?" whispered Rainolf to Aymon. But here the dwarf greeted the boys with a laugh. "Hey!" he cried. "We have been listening to your squawking,— all but Rainolf there,—he sings fairly well,—but as for the rest of you I thought some angry cats had climbed in at the windows and were fighting it out inside! But my friend here says he knows that Italian teacher of yours and that he is so fine that no matter how badly you bellow now, by and by you will all sing like a parcel of blue-birds. So cheer up!"

The old man, who had a gentle face, smiled at the speech of Malagis, and "Come, friend minstrel," said the dwarf, "sing us another song, like you sang to me a while ago, and show the youngsters what singing is!"

The boys crowded eagerly around, for everybody delighted in these wandering minstrels, or minnesingers as they were often called, and whose songs usually told some story, thus taking the place of story books which nobody had then.

The singer was from the southern part of Gaul, where they were better trained than in the ruder parts of the kingdom, and they all listened with pleasure as he touched the strings of his instrument and sang several song-stories in a voice still sweet and mellow, though he was no longer young.

Presently, after he had paused to rest awhile, "Won't you sing us another, sir minstrel?" begged Rainolf.

"I am a little tired, lad," answered the minstrel, "for before I fell in with your friend Malagis here, I had been practicing my song about Roland and the battle of Roncesvalles, which is my most difficult piece."

"Well," said Malagis, pursing his lips and shaking his head, "you had better leave that out of your list, my friend, if you want to sing in the palace before King Charlemagne, as I believe you said you did."

"Why," said the minstrel with a disappointed look, "it is my best song, and I thought he would like it. It is a favorite subject with the minnesingers where I come from. The Pass of Roncesvalles is not so very far from my home."

"That may be," said Malagis firmly, "but you don't know the King. He has never gotten over the loss of his nephew Roland and all the brave Paladins with him, and has never been quite the same since that battle. So I advise you to choose some other subject for him."

"But, sir minstrel," put in one of the boys, "won't you tell us the story? We won't ask you to sing it if you are tired, but just tell it. Of course we've heard of Roland and the Pass of Roncesvalles, but we'd like to hear what you have to say about it."

But the story will make a chapter all to itself.

CHAPTER VII: The Minnesinger Tells of Roland

"I DARE say," began the minstrel, "you know it all happened more than twenty years ago. King Charlemagne with a great army had gone down to Spain to fight the Saracens there, who were heathens ruled by the Emir Marsilius. With Charlemagne were his twelve Paladins, the noblest and bravest knights of the realm; and among them the bravest of all was young Roland, the King's nephew."

"Did you see Roland, sir?" asked Rainolf eagerly. "Malagis remembers him and says he was the handsomest knight he ever saw, and that he had more adventures than anybody else and had even spent a while in fairyland!" To which Malagis gravely nodded his head.

"Why, yes," said the minstrel, with a rather bewildered look, "I didn't know about his being in fairyland, but maybe he had, for everybody said he had had a wonderful life. I saw the whole army as it went by on the way to Spain; for my home is near the Pyrenees Mountains which divide Spain from Gaul. It was a great sight, the King in his iron armor riding a prancing war-horse and carrying a huge lance, and following him thousands of soldiers with spears and shields and banners and trumpets. The twelve Paladins rode together, Roland side by side with Oliver, his brother-in-arms."

"Malagis said they had been best friends ever since they were little boys!" said Aymon. "True," said the minstrel, "and a noble pair they were. Hanging from Roland's shoulder by a golden chain I saw the gleam of his ivory horn Olivant. I suppose you know about that?" and the minstrel paused inquiringly.

"O yes!" cried several of the boys. "It was the magic horn that had belonged to the King's grandfather, Charles the Hammer. It was made of the tooth of a sea-horse and all set thick with precious stones. After Charles the Hammer died nobody, not even King Charlemagne, could make the horn blow till Roland tried it one day and then it blew so loud that they heard it all the way from Aachen to Paris! So the King gave it to Roland."

"Good!" said the minstrel, while Malagis nodded approvingly. "And I suppose it's no use to tell you about his sword Durandal, either?"

"Yes," said the boys, "we know the King gave that to Roland too, and it was one Trojan Hector wore. It was the sharpest sword in the world."

"Was it any finer than King Charlemagne's sword?" asked Rainolf. "Isn't Joyeuse very wonderful?"

"Joyeuse is indeed a wonderful sword," answered Malagis. "Folks say that forged in it is the tip of the spear that pierced our Saviour's side. I don't know whether that is so or not, but it is a very terrible weapon. Though, for that matter," he added, "any weapon would be terrible enough in the hands of King Charlemagne. But," he said turning to the minstrel, "go on with your tale. It agrees very well with what I have always told these youngsters here."

"So," went on the minstrel, "Charlemagne crossed the Pyrenees and marched into Spain. After some very hard fighting he captured a number of Saracen cities, and in one of them, Cordova, he decided to rest awhile. While he was there messengers came from the Emir saying their master was anxious for peace, and that if the Franks would go back to Gaul, Marsilius would soon come to Aachen and swear homage to Charlemagne and be baptized as a Christian. He offered rich presents as pledges of his good faith if the King would send a favorable answer.

"When Charlemagne asked the Paladins what they thought about it, all but Roland and Oliver advised him to make peace."

"You haven't said anything about Ganelon, the traitor, sir!" said Rainolf.

"Give me time, lad!" replied the minstrel. "I was just coming to him. I suppose you know he was the one the King sent back with the messengers to say he would make peace and to receive the pledges from Marsilius; though, of course, Charlemagne had no idea how false-hearted Ganelon was."

"And Ganelon hated Roland, too, didn't he?" interrupted one of the boys.

"Yes," said the minstrel, "he was a miserable traitor; and when he went to the Emir and Marsilius offered him a sum of gold if he would help plan how to destroy Charlemagne's army, he eagerly agreed. Though he knew Marsilius could never conquer the whole army, he showed him how he might trap a part of it in which would be Roland and most of the bravest knights.

"Then he went back to Cordova with the rich presents from the Emir and told the King everything was all right and Marsilius would do as he promised.

"So Charlemagne started back to Gaul. He did not expect any trouble, but, as every wise commander does on leaving a country where enemies might be lurking, he placed a strong guard at the back of his army. In this rear guard were the good Archbishop Turpin, who was as good a fighter as a bishop, the Paladins, and twenty thousand fighting men, all led by Roland.

"After several days' marching, King Charlemagne leading the main army climbed over the rocky peaks of the Pyrenees and entered Gaul; only the rear guard was still making its way through the mountain valleys and steep narrow passes."

"Then they heard the Saracens' trumpets!" broke in one of the boys; for they all knew the story and always grew excited in the telling.

"Yes," said the minstrel, "all at once they heard a terrible blast of trumpets, and Oliver sprang from his horse and climbed to the top of a tall pine tree to try to see where the enemy was. He looked in all directions, and then he came down and said that never had he seen so great a host of Saracens! Their bright spears were gleaming on all sides; for, as Ganelon had planned, they had followed the rear guard and trapped them in the narrowest pass of the Pyrenees where it would be hardest for the Franks to defend themselves."

"We know!" cried Aymon. "It was the Pass of Roncesvalles!"—which means in our language the Valley of Thorns, and remember this; for everybody nowadays is expected to know about Roland and the Valley of Thorns just as much as those boys listening to the old minstrel over eleven hundred years ago.

"In a moment," went on the minstrel, "they heard the trumpets sounding nearer; and then Oliver, who had seen that the Saracens out-numbered the rear guard at least ten to one, begged Roland to blow his wonderful horn Olivant so that King Charlemagne might hear and come back to help them."

"But Roland was too brave!" exclaimed Rainolf.

"True," said the minstrel, "he was too brave and proud, and scorned to blow his horn for help against the heathens. Three times Oliver begged him, but each time he refused. Then the good Archbishop Turpin raised his hands and blessed all the men; for none of them hoped to escape alive. When he had finished, he drew his own sword with the rest and soon the Saracens rushed upon them and the fight began. Long and terrible was the battle, and bravely did the Frankish heroes defend themselves; but at length, one by one, all had fallen before the spears of the Saracens, save only Roland and Oliver and the good Archbishop, and they, too, were mortally wounded.

"Then at last Roland raised Olivant to his lips and with his dying breath blew a long blast; not hoping for help, for it was now too late, but because the Archbishop wished that Charlemagne might come and bear their bodies away from the wolves and wild beasts.

The blast echoed through the mountains, loud and clear and piercing, till far away in Gaul King Charlemagne heard it and knew that something terrible had happened, and quickly he turned about and hastened back over the Pyrenees. He ordered all his trumpeters to keep sounding their trumpets so that when they drew near Roland would know they were coming.

"But the King's army had far to march, and long before it reached the Pass of Roncesvalles all lay dead there save Roland. Then he staggered to his feet, and taking in his hand his wonderful sword Durandal, with a last effort he struck its blade against a mighty rock."

"Why did he do that?" asked Rainolf.

"Because," answered the minstrel, "he thought he would rather destroy Durandal than have it fall into the hands of the heathen. But instead of Durandal breaking, it was the great rock that split, for nothing could turn the edge of that magic blade. Four times Roland struck with Durandal, but each time bright and shining he drew it from a fresh cleft in the stone,—and I have seen those clefts myself," declared the minstrel, "so I know it is true! Then Roland lay down on the grass and placing Durandal and Olivant under his body, he held up his right hand to God, and so died the hero."

Everybody was very still for a few minutes. Then presently one of the boys said, "Malagis says that King Charlemagne cried when he came back and found Roland and all the brave Paladins and everybody dead."

WITH HIS DYING BREATH BLEW A LONG BLAST.

"Indeed he did!" said Malagis. "One of the soldiers who was with the army told me the King cried bitterly. And no wonder! It was a terrible blow to lose all his bravest knights, and he was immensely fond of Roland."

"Where did they bury Roland?" asked the minstrel. "I never quite knew."

"At the Abbey of Blaye," answered Malagis. "Charlemagne had Roland and Oliver and the Archbishop laid there in beautiful white marble tombs."

"Please," inquired Rainolf, "what became of Durandal and Olivant?"

"Well," said Malagis slowiy, "the King took the horn Olivant and filled it with gold and sent it to the church at Bordeaux where it may be seen in front of the altar."

"And Durandal?" again asked Rainolf.

But Malagis, who did not know about the end of Durandal (nor does anybody else), pretended not to hear; and jumping down from the stone seat, "Upon my word!" he cried. "Why, it is past dinner time! Come on, sir minstrel, and try the palace fare. The King will give you welcome when the hunt is over."

So they all went over to the palace; and late in the day the hunters rode back with two great boars. These had fought viciously when brought to bay, and killed three hounds with their sharp tusks and badly wounded one of the huntsmen; so the hunt was considered to have been a great success. King Charlemagne was in high spirits, and after supper everybody went into the palace hall where they listened to the minstrel as he sang his song-stories. The King praised him much, for heeding the advice of Malagis, he was wise enough to leave out the one about Roland.

CHAPTER VIII: Presents for the King

ONE afternoon late in the summer all the children of Aachen were racing and chasing through its crooked streets and looking eagerly down the long road beyond that stretched away to the south. Even the grown folks were coming to their doors and standing as if they expected to see something.

Soon Rainolf and the palace pages came hurrying along, and as they passed a black-beamed house where an old man was blinking at the window, "Master Leobard," said Rainolf, "do you know when they are coming?"

"No, lad," answered the old astrologer, "but the stars say the King is to receive a present soon, so I dare say it will be along by and by." And muttering to himself he went back to tending a fire in a queer earthen stove where in some curious vessels he was trying, as did many people then, to make gold out of something else and, of course, not succeeding.

"Master Leobard says the stars told him," laughed one of the boys, "but maybe the runner that came to the palace last night had fresher news."

"Where did that runner come from?" asked another.

"I think from the nearest town south of here," said Aymon. "You know he came to tell the King some people are on the way here bringing him something, I didn't hear what."

"I guess he told all the town folks, too," said Rainolf, "from the way they are on the look-out!"

By this time they had come to the edge of Aachen. "Let's go down the road a piece," said Aymon. "Surely they will have to come this way."

So on they loitered past little thatched huts here and there in the fields, where the peasant folk lived. Presently, "I'm thirsty!" said one of the boys; "let's go over to that hut and get a drink."

When they reached it and looked in at the door a gust of smoke blew in their faces from an open fire on the bare earthen floor. Over this was an iron pot full of thin soup which a woman was stirring with one hand as she held in her arms a shock-headed baby dressed in homespun. At one side of the room were two or three wooden troughs filled with straw which were the family beds. In the middle of the floor a block of wood made from the stump of a tree did for table and came handy also when they needed to cut bread, which was always so coarse and hard that when they wanted any the father usually had to chop off pieces with his ax.

When the boys asked the woman for a drink, she handed them a gourd and pointed toward a tree in a near-by field; and scampering over there they found a spring of good water. When they returned the gourd, "Aren't you going over to the road?" asked Aymon.

But she only stared at him without answering. For the Frankish peasants knew but little beyond ploughing the fields with their rude ploughs and toiling for a bare living. And the hut was not poorer than most of the others dotting the country.

But the boys had already hurried off, for "Look!" cried Rainolf, pointing down the road, "there they come!"

Sure enough, a number of people were coming toward them. Some were riding spirited Arabian horses and some walking, all had black eyes and hair, quite different from the Franks, and all had on large turbans and flowing robes such as people wear in the Far East. Some were leading pack-horses with bulging saddle-bags, but in the midst of them came the most amazing thing of all! It was a huge animal with a wrinkly gray skin, wide flapping ears, little shrewd black eyes, and thick legs with toes like the scallops of an enormous pinking-iron—but hear the boys,

"Do look at that *outlandish* beast!"

"What on earth do you suppose it is?"

"Is that a *tail* hanging where its mouth belongs? Look! Look! how it keeps curling it up and poking it around!"

"My, but that's a grand red seat on its back!"

"Wouldn't you think that man with the queer clothes would tumble out? See how it rocks when the beast walks!"

"Do you think the man is guiding it with that long wand, or do you suppose he is a magician?"

"Pshaw!" you say. "Why, it was just a circus procession, and didn't those silly boys know an *elephant* when they saw it?"

Well, you are quite mistaken; for it was no circus procession even if there was an elephant in it. Indeed, none of the Franks had ever heard of such a thing as a circus; while as for elephants, most of them would have been far less surprised if a dragon had come flying out of the forest, for they knew much more about dragons—or thought they did.

No, the people coming along the road were messengers from Haroun-al-Raschid, the great Caliph of Bagdad, ever and ever so far away in Asia. (If you have read your Arabian Nights stories you know all about the great Caliph; and, if you don't know, you had best hurry up and find out.) Now, Haroun-al-Raschid and the mighty Charlemagne, though they had never met, were very good friends and admired each other greatly. Some time before, the King had sent messengers bearing handsome presents and good wishes to the Caliph. It had taken over three years to reach Bagdad, for it was then a long and dangerous journey; while they were there the Caliph, who wished after a while to send gifts in return, asked them what they thought the King would like, and they said they knew one thing Charlemagne wanted dreadfully and that was an elephant.

So, by and by, when Haroun-al-Raschid sent his own messengers to bear presents and his good wishes to the King, he remembered about the elephant and took care to send an extra big fine one. And at last, after a long long journey, here it was tramping along the road almost to Aachen!

Of course the boys all ran along behind as the procession wound through the town, the strangers looking curiously about, the Arab horses daintily picking their way over the rough stones, and the elephant lumbering steadily along and all the while peering around with his sharp little eyes.

And how the town folks said, "Oh!" and "Ah!" and "What *do* you think that queer animal is?" till they reached the palace where the strangers dismounted in the courtyard. They unpacked the bulging saddle-bags which were full of presents, and with these in their arms they were taken to the great hall of the palace where Charlemagne received them with kindness and honor. And soon he himself came out to see the wonderful elephant, which seemed to delight him more than anything else.

The boys stayed around as close as they dared, and, when presently, the elephant was led off to a special stall in the royal stables, they followed.

"What a magnificent embroidered cloth that is hanging over his back!" said Rainolf.

"Yes," said another boy, "those pearls and jewels sewed on it must have cost a lot!"

"How do you suppose he eats, with that queer tail on his mouth?" said Ayrron. "Let's watch what they feed him."

And they had great fun seeing everything that was done for him and getting acquainted with the Bagdad elephant, who was to live in Aachen for nine years and be the chief pride of Charlemagne in all the royal processions of the time. He was even to go to war with him and carry the King's own baggage on his broad back.

Meantime, while the boys were off in the stables, the other rich presents sent by the Caliph were being displayed and discussed by everybody.

"Have you seen the wonderful clock?" said one to another.

"No, what is a clock?"

"It is something that tells the time of day!"

"Is it anything like our sun-dials or hour-glasses? "

"Not a bit! It is a kind of machine that runs by water. It is shaped like a tower with twelve windows, and they say that each hour the windows open and bronze horsemen ride out and then ride in again!"

"How wonderful!"

"Yes, and there are splendid silks and gold embroideries, too, for the Queen and Princesses!"

"And such beautiful chess-men for the King to play with! They are men riding on animals like the one that came to-day and are all carved from ivory!"

"Oh, yes, and a wonderful silk tent, too! Big enough for dozens of men, but so fine I believe you could squeeze it up and carry it in your fist!"

So the tongues wagged, and, you may be sure, neither Rainolf nor any of the other boys missed seeing a single thing.

CHAPTER IX: Rainolf in the Writing-Room

THERE was one part of the palace in which Rainolf especially delighted, and this was the great writing-room. Here, always, were to be found a number of monks from the monastery by the cathedral who spent their time making the most beautiful books. It was chiefly the Bible and the works of the older Greek and Latin authors which they carefully copied out by hand so more people might read them. And all the while they were learning more and more how to decorate and make them beautiful with gold and color.

The King admired these beautiful painted books above all things, and in every way encouraged the monks to make them finer and finer. And they grew so skillful all over his kingdom that the painted, or illuminated books, as they were called, which were made during the reign of Charlemagne are still treasured and admired by everybody.

Rainolf used to spend an hour or two every day in this writing-room, for one of the monks, Brother Coplas, was teaching him to write, and he hoped some day to learn to paint also, for he longed to make a beautiful book all himself. And down in his heart he looked forward to the day when one of the books he made would be filled with his own songs. For all the while Master Einhard was helping him with his music and even encouraging him to make up little songs to sing.

Rainolf was thinking of this as he was busy at work in the writing-room a few days after the coming of the Caliph's messengers, when the door opened and in came the King. With him were two of the Bagdad strangers whom he had brought to see the writing-room, of which he was very proud. The visitors looked with interest at the queer high desks where the monks were working, at the rolls of parchment and the paints and gold and colored inks and goose-quill pens.

"Father Willibrod," said the King to the head of the writing-room, "will you not show us some of the finished pages?"

Father Willibrod hastened to open a great drawer in a desk nearby and displayed a number of large pages so beautifully written and surrounded by such brilliant and glowing borders of birds and flowers with here and there pictures on backgrounds of sparkling gold all so lovely that the strangers exclaimed with admiration and the King smiled with pleasure.

"Show us some of the covers, too, Father Willibrod," he said.

And in another drawer they saw covers already finished ready for the painted pages. For the finest books these covers were of wrought silver set with precious stones, and some of beautifully carved ivory. Others were of velvet, which had been embroidered by the ladies of the palace; while for the commoner books deer-skin would be used.

As the party was leaving the room, the King passed near the desk where Brother Coplas and Rainolf sat side by side. He paused a moment looking at the boy's work and "Good!" he said, "You are improving, lad," and then he sighed as he added, "I wish I had had such training when my hand was supple as yours!"

As he passed out Brother Coplas whispered to Rainolf, "The King would give anything to be able to write and paint books!"

"Why, he can write, can't he?" asked Rainolf in surprise.

"To be sure," said Brother Coplas. "But he wants to be able to do it evenly and regularly as we do in our books. One of his body servants told me he keeps a pen and tablet of parchment under his pillow every night, and often when he can't sleep he will get up and have a lamp lighted and will practice for a long time trying to write beautifully."

And this was not so easy, either; for writing then was more like printing, each letter being made separately, which, of course, was much slower than our way of joining them together; a simple little trick which no one as yet had thought of.

Before long Rainolf had finished his page, and as his fingers were tired he got up and strolled around the room, for he loved to look at what they were all doing.

"Oh, but that is beautiful!" he exclaimed as he stopped by a desk where a monk was writing a chapter from the Bible in letters of gold on a page of parchment he had stained a rich purple.

*A MONK WAS WRITING A CHAPTER FROM THE BIBLE IN
LETTERS OF GOLD.*

"Master Alcuin says they have nothing finer in Tours," said another brother, who had paused to admire the page, "and in his monastery they do famous work."

"Yes," said Rainolf, "Brother Coplas told me Master Alcuin is having a wonderful Bible made there for the King."

"Why," he said, as he came to another desk, "I didn't know you were here, Master Einhard! What is this you are writing? It isn't Latin!"

"No," answered Master Einhard, who was carefully copying on neat pages something written on a number of loose scraps. "It is some work I am doing for the King, and I am writing it in our own language; for these are songs of some of the Frankish minnesingers. You know how the King likes songs."

"I know he likes yours!" said Rainolf warmly.

"Perhaps," said Master Einhard modestly. "But he likes other peoples', too. Sometimes, when minnesingers come on long winter evenings, he will have the fireplace filled with blazing logs and will wrap himself up in a big mantle of otter skins and sit up half the night listening to them. Some of these men come from the wilder parts of the kingdom up north, and they know old heathen song-stories that have been handed down nobody knows how long. The King is wonderfully interested in these, and whenever any of those people come he gets me to write down the words of the stories they sing, and as, of course, I have to write very fast, it needs to be copied plainly. I have written out ever so many, and the King is getting quite a collection." Here he pointed with pride to a pile of pages in a recess of his desk.

As Rainolf passed on, Master Einhard again bent over his work; for he could not possibly know that twenty years later, when King Charlemagne was dead and gone, his stupid son Louis would one day find those carefully written pages and, not dreaming of their value, would carelessly toss them in the fire!

Heigho! it is a great pity to be stupid!

Meantime, as Rainolf left the writing-room and went into the courtyard he almost ran into Malagis, who was standing on the toes of his good foot and whirling around like a weather-cock.

"Hey, youngster!" he said, "I was just taking some exercise. By the way, I have news for you. Didn't your horoscope say you were to see something of the world?"

"Yes," said Rainolf, puzzled.

"Well, I guess all of our stars must say the same thing, for we are all likely to go traveling."

"How?" asked Rainolf.

"Listen!" answered Malagis, pointing, with a wise air, to the highest palace tower. "Didn't I tell you youngsters a while ago that that big bronze eagle was turning a tiny bit to the south? And didn't I say it meant the King would be needed in that direction, most likely in Italy?"

"Yes, you did," answered Rainolf respectfully.

"Well," said Malagis, with a triumphant gleam in his strange bright eyes, "look at it now!"

As Rainolf gazed, with an awed expression, sure enough, the great bronze bird had veered more and more till it seemed to be looking straight to the south.

"Now, sir," said Malagis, "I happen to know that the King has received word that Pope Leo is in trouble in Rome and wants the most powerful king in Christendom—of course that's Charlemagne— to come and help him. And the King is going, and, as usual, when he can possibly manage it, he will take nearly everybody along. So there! What did I tell you!"

And Malagis again began his whirling, while Rainolf stared at the eagle with his head full of eager dreams.

CHAPTER X: Christmas Day of the Year 800

IT was quite true, as Malagis had said, Charlemagne was going to Italy early in the autumn and was to take most of his household with him. The household, however, was used to moving about with the King from palace to palace, and even when at war he often took his family and the school along. So everybody knew just how to arrange things.

But as this story must end with this very chapter, I cannot begin to tell you about all these preparations; of the army which, of course, must be got ready, of the ox-carts and ox-carts full of baggage, of the horses for the men to ride, the ponies for the pages and the covered wagons with embroidered scarlet curtains and cushions for the ladies, of the quantities of food, and the thousand and one things that must go along when a lot of people set out to travel.

Neither can I stop to tell how they started off and all the interesting and wonderful things which Rainolf and the palace pages saw as they rode along with the great cavalcade. At the town of Mainz they crossed the River Rhine on a wooden bridge with stone piers, which the King had caused to be built a few years before, and everybody thought it most remarkable! And no wonder, for it was the only real bridge in all the Frankish kingdom; at other places they had only boats to cross rivers.

On, on, they went, always southward; and, by and by, up, up, they clambered over the towering white peaks of the Alps Mountains, round precipices that made Rainolf and his companions fairly hold their breath, and then at last down, down, into the lovely land of Italy with its blue skies and olive and orange trees and its cities with such beautiful castles and palaces and churches that again the boys caught their breath, but this time with wonder and admiration. And you would have gasped, too, if you had been a Frankish boy used only to Aachen and the wild forests around it, and if you had always thought the King's palace and the cathedral the two finest buildings in all the world!

Indeed, Rainolf and the rest of the pages found out a great many things on that journey; and when they drew near to the ancient city of Rome they began to realize what it was to be in a country that had been civilized hundreds of years before. But we cannot stop to hear all the things they did, nor of how at length Pope Leo with his bishops and cardinals came to meet King Charlemagne and together they entered imperial Rome, all the great cavalcade following close behind.

Rainolf and Aymon and the other boys were quite silent as they rode through the streets of the famous city. They had seen so much and exclaimed so much on the way, that they had used up all the wonder adjectives they knew, and Rainolf scarcely answered when Malagis, who rode a little piebald pony beside him, poked him with his wand with "Well, boy, Aachen will look a bit tame when we go back, hey?"

Malagis had been in Rome once before with the King, and he now began to point out this and that wonderful place, till they reached the beautiful marble palace where the King was to stay with his family and many of his nobles and closest attendants, among these Malagis and Rainolf his cup-bearer. Aymon and the other boys and the rest of the household were lodged in palaces near by.

It is too bad we have not time to talk about the splendid feasts for the King, for they lasted for seven days, and at all of them Rainolf stood behind his chair, and it is not likely he missed anything that went on. Then, after the feasting, King Charlemagne set himself to see to the matters which had brought him to Rome; and the end of it was he delivered Pope Leo from the enemies who had been plotting against him.

By this time it was very near Christmas, and this is the great day we have been hurrying up to reach; for it was to be a tremendously important one in the life of Charlemagne, and, indeed, in the history of the world, and we cannot possibly finish this story without telling about it.

Very early in the morning everybody in Rome crowded toward the great church of Saint Peter for the Christmas service. All who could, squeezed in, and hundreds and hundreds, who couldn't, stood in the large square outside. A place within had been reserved for the King's household, or Rainolf, who came with Master Einhard and a number of other Franks, would never have had a spot to stand.

As they made their way through the throng, they noticed that the faces of the Roman people all showed a curious air of expectancy. There seemed to be a feeling everywhere that something unusual was going to happen.

51

Rainolf felt it, and wondered, as he looked around the church which was the most splendid sight imaginable. Gold and jewels and mosaics glittered everywhere, and between the lofty marble columns of the long aisles hung curtains of the richest purple velvet which were brought out only on the grandest occasions.

These partly shut out the light gleaming dimly through the windows of clouded glass, but hundreds of tall wax tapers shone brightly and at the eastern end of the church, high over the altar, a dazzle of golden light hung from golden chains.

"Oh, Master Einhard," whispered Rainolf, "what is that beautiful thing?"

"That is called the 'Pharos,'" said Master Einhard. "It is a candelabrum of pure gold, and they say it holds three thousand candles. I was here once before but I never saw it lighted, for it is only for great celebrations. Isn't it splendid! And look at the beautiful triumphal arch over it! I think that is new for to-day."

Here Rainolf breathed another long "Oh!" and so did Master Einhard; for just then some of the crowd in front of them moved a little so they could see between. And there, directly under the blazing Pharos and the triumphal arch, shone the wonderful shrine of the Apostle Peter in whose honor the church had been named. The shrine was covered with plates of gold and silver and studded with jewels; mosaics in all the colors of the rainbow glittered around it, and on the steps in front of it was a majestic kneeling figure.

For a moment Rainolf stared in silence; then turning to Master Einhard with a bewildered look, "Is it—can it be King Charlemagne?"

"Yes," replied Master Einhard in a low voice, "it could be no other."

It was indeed the King; though no wonder Rainolf was puzzled, for instead of wearing the familiar Frankish dress, he was clad as a Roman noble of the highest rank. A wide mantle of pure white wool bordered with royal purple covered him with its many folds and was held at one shoulder by a jeweled golden clasp. On his feet were sandals laced with golden cords.

It was a splendid picture; and as the King continued to kneel with bowed head, all eyes were fixed upon him, still with that curious look of expectancy. In a moment a hush fell everywhere, for Pope Leo and his attendant priests had entered. All wore magnificent robes stiff with gold embroidery and precious stones, and after them came choir-boys in lace and velvet, swinging clouds of sweet incense from beautifully jeweled censers, and the solemn mass began.

At a pause in the service, "Master Einhard," whispered Rainolf softly, "what is it? I feel as if something great is going to happen." Indeed, this feeling, which had been in the air all the morning, seemed to grow stronger with everybody.

"I do not know," whispered Master Einhard slowly, "but—I believe— King Charlemagne will leave this church something different—"

But again the sound of chanting rose and fell; and then, by and by, the last notes, one by one, died away, the clouds of fragrant incense dissolved faintly in the quiet air, there was a moment of intense silence, and then just as King Charlemagne was about to rise from his knees, suddenly Pope Leo stood before him holding in his hands a golden crown. With a swift movement he placed this on the King's head, and at the same instant, as if by magic, thousands of voices rang out, "To Charles the Augustus, crowned of God, the great and pacific Emperor, long life and victory!" which was the ancient greeting with which the Roman people were accustomed to hail their Emperors. Then, led by Pope Leo, everybody sang a hymn asking all the saints to bless the new Emperor, his children and his subjects.

"What—what does it all mean?" asked Rainolf, when he could get his breath for bewilderment.

"It means," slowly answered Master Einhard, who had been keenly watching everything, "that our Frankish King Charlemagne is now also Emperor of the Roman Empire and the greatest monarch in all Christendom."

"But," said Rainolf, still puzzled, "I thought he was the greatest monarch before?"

"Yes," said Master Einhard, "he was; and what is left of the ancient Roman Empire has for years looked to him to defend it from its enemies; yet really to wear the crown as Emperor means a glory and power nothing else can quite give. You will understand better by and by, lad."

As to what King,—no, we forget,—*Emperor* Charlemagne himself thought about it all, nobody will ever be quite sure. Perhaps in his wisdom he foresaw how for centuries after his own time, when the Roman Empire had ceased to be either Roman or even an empire, the kings who followed him would still strive to be crowned Emperor as he had been and there would be much war and bloodshed because of it. Perhaps he dimly guessed something of this, for after the coronation was over, though he accepted all its responsibility, nevertheless he declared that he would never have gone to Saint Peter's Church that Christmas morning had he known what Pope Leo meant to do.

But whether he knew about it beforehand or not, there he was that Christmas Day of the year 800 leaving Saint Peter's with the Roman crown glittering on his head. And having thus seen our noble King Charlemagne made into an Emperor, our story must end.

Good-by, Rainolf! Good-by, Aymon, and Malagis and Masters Einhard and Alcuin and all the rest!—And would you really like to know what became of some of them? Well, Rainolf's horoscope worked out fairly true. When troubles came to him he met them manfully, and always when needed for the Frankish wars he proved a good and loyal soldier; but always, too, as Master Leobard had said, there was something else for which he cared much more. It was his songs. And as he grew older his voice grew sweeter still, and he and Master Einhard together used often to delight the Emperor with their singing. Rainolf, by and by, became a famous minnesinger, making up his own beautiful song-stories, and even at last fulfilling his boyish wish, he learned to paint and write so well that he made a lovely book all of his own songs.

Aymon and the other boys all turned out well, too; though none of them made a name for himself as did Rainolf.

Malagis continued to wear the yellow tunic of jester and capered good-humoredly through life; though long afterward people declared he had been a great wizard and minnesingers told no end of marvelous stories about him.

Master Einhard served faithfully as scribe as long as Charlemagne lived; and then two years later he wrote a life of the Emperor. It is not very long, but is so perfectly well done that to this day when people want to know about him first of all they look to see what Master Einhard wrote.

As for the mighty Charlemagne himself, when he died no King or Emperor ever had so wonderful a burial. He was placed in a splendid tomb in the cathedral of Aachen, seated on a marble throne, arrayed in the magnificent royal robes he had scorned to wear during life, his jeweled crown upon his head, his golden scepter in his right hand, and spread open across his knees the beautiful painted Bible made at Tours and which Master Alcuin had presented to him that famous Christmas Day.

And then, by and by, the minnesingers began to make up songs about him; and for hundreds of years more and more were made up, all of them growing more and more wonderful till the song-stories of which Charlemagne is the hero are counted today among the most beautiful in the world. And many of these minnesingers tell strange tales. Some of them even declare that the great monarch is not dead, but that fairies and wizards carried him off to a marvelous cavern in the lofty mountain of Dessenberg, and that there he sits sleeping a magical sleep, his head resting on a white marble table and his long white beard flowing to his feet. They say the mountain dwarfs guard the cavern, but that some day—some day— Charlemagne will waken! And, if he does—Oh, wouldn't you like to be there to see?

Pronounciation of Proper Names

Aachen (ah´-ken)
Aix-la-Chapelle (aks-la-sha-pel´)
Alcuin (al´-kwin)
Ay´-mon
Bag´-dad
Blaye (blay)
Bordeaux (bor-doe´)
Bur´-gun-dy
Caliph (ka´lif)
Charlemagne (char´-le-mane)
Des´sen-berg
Durandal (doo-ron-dal´)
Einhard (ine´-hard)
E´-mir
Haroun-al-Raschid (ha-roon´-al-rash´-id)
Ir´-min-sul
Mal´-a-gis
Marsilius (mar-see´-le-us)
Ol´-i-vant
Pa-der-born´
Pyrenees (pir´-e-neez)
Rain´-olf
Roncesvalles (ron-thes-val´-yas)